This book is inspired by a true story.

COVID-19 led to a lockdown in which the donkey Baldomera,
from Málaga, Spain, couldn't see her friend Ismael for two months.

When at last they could meet, the story of their
emotional encounter went viral all over the world.

The story of Baldomera has touched the hearts
of more than 50 million people.

Thank you, Ismael and Baldomera, for sharing the story of your friendship.

"Carrying anything?"
"See for yourself... White butterflies..."

Juan Ramón Jiménez, *Platero and I*

To my son Álvar; hope you will never
have to wait so much for me.
Enrique García Ballesteros

To my grandfathers and grandmothers for having taught me
to love animals and the countryside.
Ismael Fernández Arias

To Álvaro, with all my love.
Ayesha L. Rubio

*NubeOcho and the authors would like to thank
Javier García León, lawyer and communications expert,
for his help in making this project come true.*

The Story of Baldomera
Somos8 Collection

© text: Enrique García Ballesteros & Ismael Fernández Arias, 2020
© illustrations: Ayesha L. Rubio, 2020
© edition: NubeOcho, 2020
© translation: Laura Fielden, 2020
www.nubeocho.com · hello@nubeocho.com

Original Title: *La burrita Baldomera*
Text editing: Rima Noureddine, Rebecca Packard.

First Edition: April 2021
ISBN: 978-84-18133-69-5
Legal Deposit: M-22849-2020

Printed in Portugal.

THE STORY OF BALDOMERA

Enrique G. Ballesteros & Ismael F. Arias

Illustrated by
Ayesha L. Rubio

nubeOCHO

Baldomera the little donkey lived a quiet, simple and lonely life.

She would mosey through the countryside, gaze out over the mountains toward the sea, swat flies with her tail and go back to the farm to sleep.

One day, Baldomera met Ismael.

When she was with him, she did more or less the same
as before, but she didn't feel lonely anymore, because now
she had a friend.

When they sat together and looked at the beach from
the mountaintop, Baldomera and Ismael smiled at each other.
They knew they were sharing a beautiful moment of peace
and tranquility.

When night fell, Ismael would groom and feed Baldomera.
She felt safe and well cared for.

From time to time, Ismael would go away for a few days to work, but he would always return, and they would be so happy to see each other again.

Every reunion with Ismael made Baldomera feel as if she was surrounded by playful butterflies.

But one day, Ismael left and he didn't come back.

A day passed. Then another, and another.
And then a week passed. And another, and another.

The longer Baldomera waited for Ismael, the sadder and more anxious she felt. She was lonely, and she didn't understand why her friend didn't return to see her.

The little donkey Baldomera was worried. It was not like Ismael to be gone for so long.

She thought about all the things that might have happened to her friend...

Baldomera thought that Ismael might be trapped in one of those traffic jams she used to see on the highway that spoiled the view and polluted the environment. But then she realized that it had been a while since she had seen traffic jams, almost since Ismael had disappeared.

She imagined Ismael floating out to sea on a sheet of ice because the poles had warmed up and a glacier had broken apart. But then surely a helicopter would have rescued him by now, because it had been so long.

Baldomera wondered if maybe someone had taken Ismael to a hospital, sickened by the black clouds that puffed out of the factories. But it had been some time since those factories had churned out smoke.

Baldomera didn't want to imagine the worst.

But what if Ismael had forgotten about her? What if he had just gotten tired of going out to the countryside to see her, and he now had other friends to play with?

Baldomera was overcome with sadness.
After a few months, when she was just about to
stop wondering about Ismael, she saw someone
in the distance walking toward her.

Who could it be after all this time?

It was Ismael!

"Ismael, my friend, you came back!" thought Baldomera
as she raced to meet him.

"Where is my little donkey?" Ismael hugged her. "How are you?"

"Heeeeeeeee. Heeee haww. Heeee hawww," cried Baldomera.

"I´ve missed you so much, but now I´m here. Forgive me, I couldn´t come any sooner."

Baldomera couldn't stop crying from the happiness she felt. Ismael was safe, and he hadn't forgotten about her.

Now they were together again, and they would always be the best of friends.